D0854022

The Child's World of
UNDERSTANDING

Printed in the U.S.A.

Library of Congress Cataloging in Publication Data

Ziegler, Sandra, 1938–
Understanding / Sandra Ziegler
p. cm.
Originally published: c1989
ISBN 1-56766-307-9 (hardcover)
1. Empathy—Juvenile literature. 2. Children—Conduct of Life.
I. Title
Bf575.E55z54 1989
179'.9—dc19 88-23745
CIP
AC

The Child's World of UNDERSTANDING

By Sandra Ziegler • Illustrated by Mechelle Ann

THE CHILD'S WORLD

What is understanding?

Understanding is holding your cat in a way that will not hurt her.

“A little understanding” is what Mom asks you to have when you want your sister to play with you, but she has to do her homework.

When your sister spills her milk, understanding is not making fun of her.

When you are coloring eggs and your sister drips blue coloring on your best yellow egg, understanding is saying, “That’s okay. Let’s make it a polka-dot egg.”

When a friend slips and falls into a mud puddle, understanding is helping him up.

When you smile at a new girl in class, you are saying, "I know how you feel." That's understanding.

And so is hugging your friend when her parakeet dies and she cries.

When your sister strikes out and drops a fly ball, understanding is saying,"You'll do better next time."

Understanding is letting your little sister sleep with you because she thinks a monster is under her bed.

When your sister is going to miss a TV special because she promised to wash dishes, understanding is saying, “I know how you feel. I’ll help you so you will finish in time.”

When a friend can't come to your birthday party because he has the chicken pox, understanding is sending over a piece of cake and a party hat.

Understanding is knowing how someone else feels,
and then treating him as you would like to be treated.

Can you think of more ways to show understanding?